E TARPLEY N
Tarpley, Natasha.
I love my hair!

Author's Note

This is how I fell in love with my hair. When I was a little girl, my mother would often comb my hair in the evening before I went to bed. I would make myself comfortable between her knees as she rubbed sweet-smelling oil along the line of my scalp where she had parted my hair. Then she would start to comb.

Sometimes she would tell me stories to distract me from the pain of stubborn tangles. But what I enjoyed most about those evenings was being so close to my mother — the texture and sound of my hair sliding through her fingers, the different hairstyles she would create, the smell of the hair oil mixing with the lingering scent of her perfume. I loved the way we laughed and talked about the day's events, just the two of us.

Now that I am older, my mother no longer combs my hair. I found this to be very liberating at first. But once initial excitement over all the different styles I could now try began to wane, I saw that beyond the freedom lay years of struggle. I went from one phase to another with my hair: from relaxers to punk-rock spikes, from braids to barely-there short natural. Almost two years ago, I decided to grow dreadlocks. For the first time since those nights when I sat between Mom's knees, I was at peace with my hair, at home again with myself.

To my mother, Marlene,
for making my hair a house
where dreams live and grow

Special thanks also to my aunt, Gwendolyn Hilary,
for invaluable suggestions and encouragement,
and to my editor, Megan Shaw Tingley, for believing
—N. A. T.

To the Most High Creator of All Things
—E. B. L.

Text copyright © 1998 by Natasha Anastasia Tarpley
Illustrations copyright © 1998 by E. B. Lewis

Little, Brown and Company

Hachette Book Group
237 Park Avenue, New York, NY 10017
Visit our website at www.lb-kids.com

Little, Brown and Company is a division of Hachette Book Group, Inc.
The Little, Brown name and logo are trademarks of Hachette Book Group, Inc.

The publisher is not responsible for websites (or their content) that are not owned by the publisher.

First Paperback Edition: September 2001
Originally published in hardcover in February 1998 by Little, Brown and Company

Library of Congress Cataloging-in-Publication Data

Tarpley, Natasha Anastasia.
    I love my hair! / by Natasha Anastasia Tarpley; illustrated by E. B. Lewis—
1st ed.
        p.   cm.
    Summary: A young African-American girl describes the different, wonderful ways she can wear her hair.
    ISBN 978-0-316-52275-5 (hc) / ISBN 978-0-316-52375-2 (pb)

12

SC

Manufactured in China

I Love My Hair!

by

Natasha Anastasia Tarpley

Illustrated by

E. B. Lewis

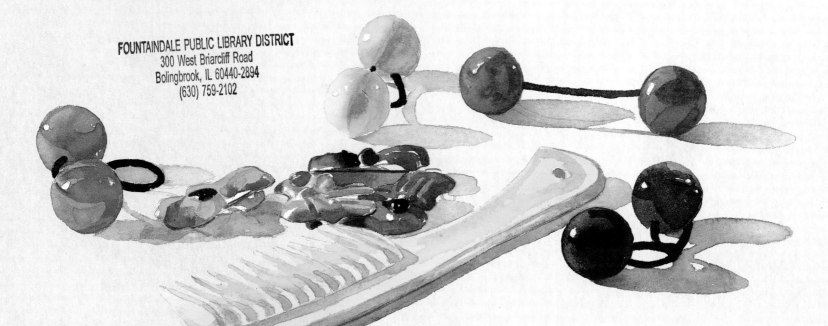

LITTLE, BROWN AND COMPANY

New York Boston

Every night before I go to bed, Mama combs my hair.
I sit between her knees,
resting my elbows on her thighs, like pillows.

Mama is always gentle.
She rubs coconut oil along my scalp
and slowly pulls the comb through my hair,
but sometimes it still hurts.

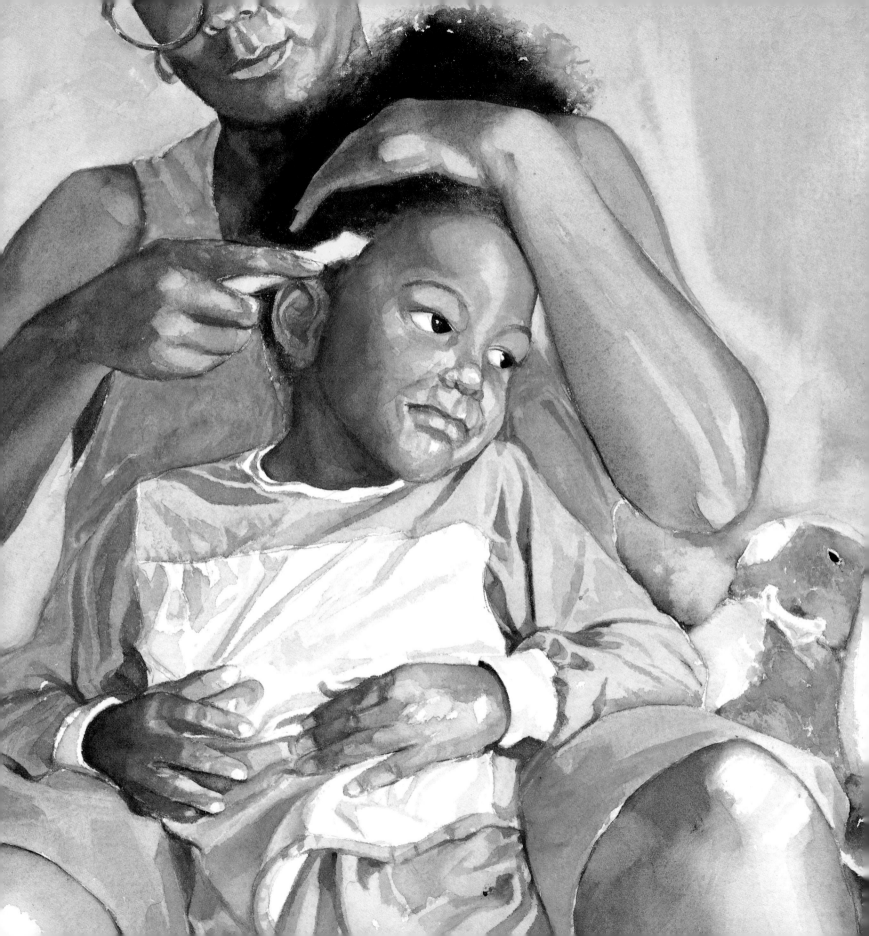

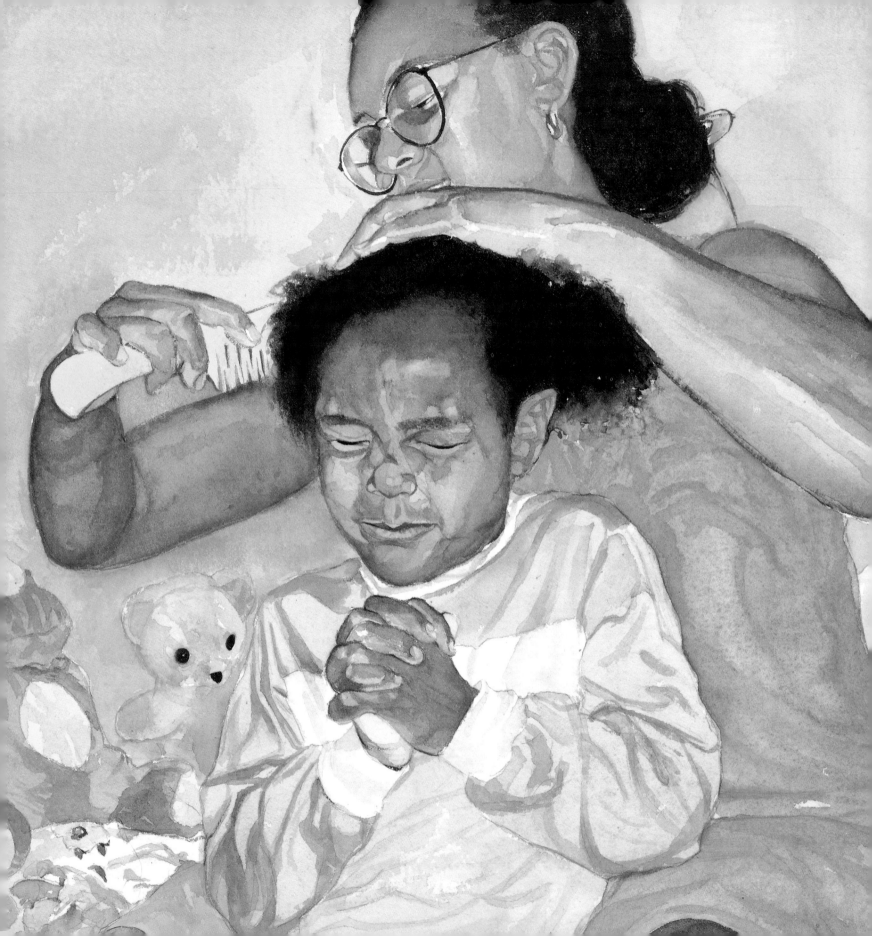

When Mama gets to especially tangled places,
I try my hardest not to cry, sucking in my breath
and pressing my hands together until they're red.

But a few tears always manage to squeeze out.

"Mama, stop!" I cry when I can't stand the comb tugging at my hair any longer.

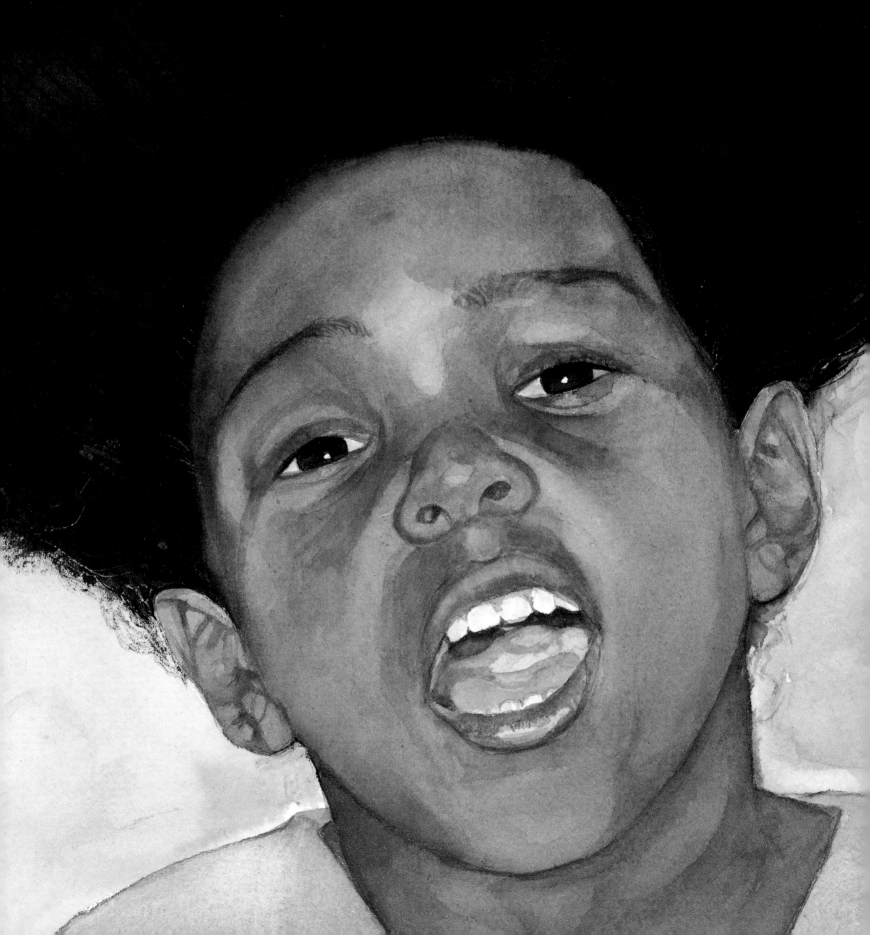

Mama puts the comb down
and rubs my hurting places.
Then she leans in close to me,
like she has a big secret to tell.
"Do you know why you're so lucky
to have this head of hair, Keyana?" she asks.
I shake my head no.
"Because it's beautiful
and you can wear it in any style you choose."

"I can spin your hair into fine, soft yarn,
just like our grandmothers did at their spinning wheels,
and weave it into a puffy little bun.

"Or I can part your hair into straight lines
and plant rows of braids along your scalp,
the way we plant seeds in our garden,
then wait and watch for them to grow."

In the morning, before we walk to the store,
Mama adds colorful beads to the ends of my braids.
The beads click to the rhythm of my walk,
helping me remember what we're going to buy:
Tap! Tap! Clicky-clacky!
Milk, bread, peanut butter.

Folks on the street look at me and smile
as I dance along to the *Tap! Tap! Clicky-clacky!*
music my hair makes just for me.

Some days I just let my hair be free
to do what it wants, to go any which-way it pleases.
Then my hair surrounds my head, like a globe.
This is my Afro style.

Once when I wore it,
the kids at school teased me.
My head felt heavy
and I let it hang down low.

But my teacher made me feel better.
She said that when she was growing up,
folks counted their hair as a blessing.
Wearing an Afro was a way for them
to stand up for what they believed,
to let the world know that they were proud
of who they were and where they came from.

I love my hair
because it is thick as a forest,
soft as cotton candy,
and curly as a vine winding upward,
reaching the sky
and climbing toward outer space.

Today I'm wearing it in my favorite style of all:
two ponytails that stick out on either side of my head
and flap in the air like a pair of wings.

One of these days I just might take off
and fly!